For my mother

KESTREL BOOKS

Published by Penguin Books Ltd, Harmondsworth, Middlesex, England

Copyright © 1984 by Jan Ormerod

First published in 1984

Printed in Great Britain by William Clowes and Sons Ltd, Beccles

British Library Cataloguing in Publication Data

Ormerod, Jan
  101 things to do with a baby.
  1. Infants – Care and hygiene – Juvenile
  literature
  I. Title
  649'.122   RJ101

ISBN 0-7226-5929-6

101 Things to do
with a Baby

JAN ORMEROD

Kestrel Books

1 say good morning

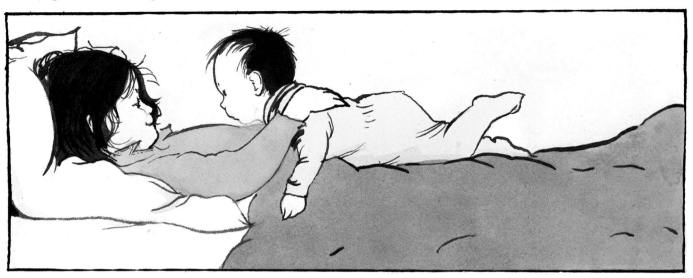

2 play with baby before breakfast

3 put him in his special chair

4 give him cereal

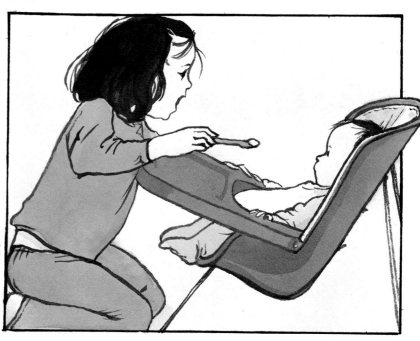

5 and let him share your egg

6 better clean him up

7 let's do the washing

8 put it in the machine

9 add the soap powder

10 watch it whizz around

11 spy him in his bouncing chair

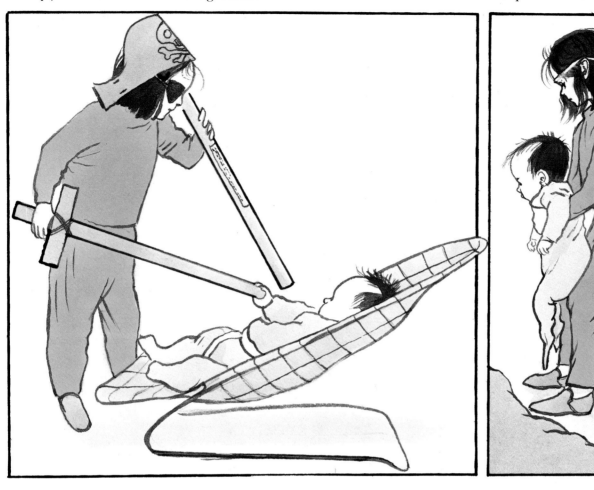

12 put him on the floor

13 for a chat

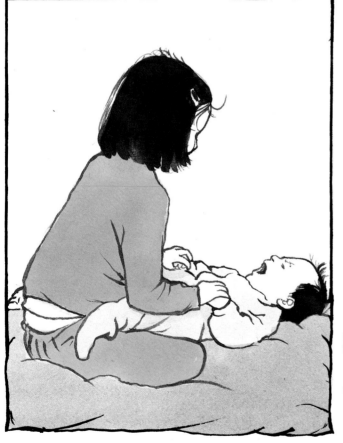

14 exercise his legs

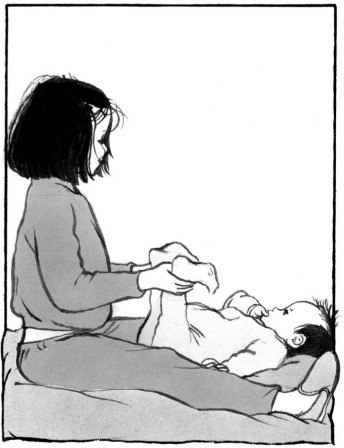

15 now do sit ups

16 or stand ups

17 or push ups

18 see how we can stretch

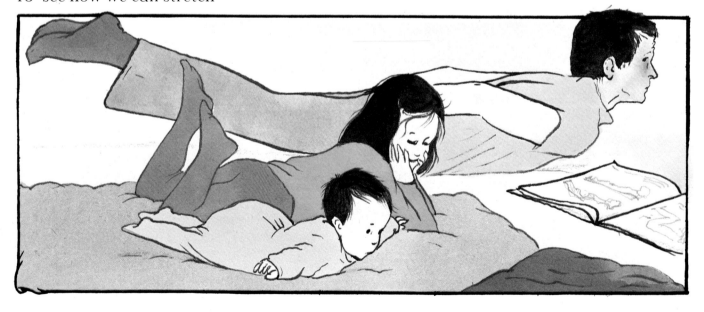

19 twist left

20 twist right

21 and roll over

22 now knees up all together

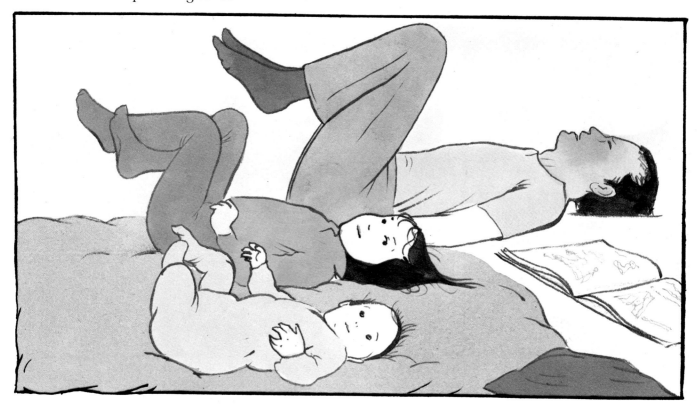

23 and then relax

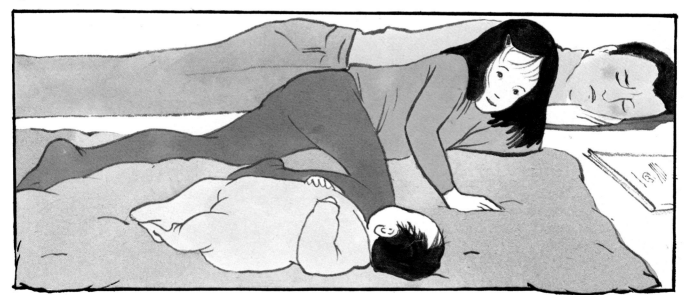

24 put on rubber boots   25 and a plastic apron   26 get the mop

27 the baby's bath   28 and a nice soft towel

29 not too hot

30 put in the bubbles

31 froth them up

32 put in the baby

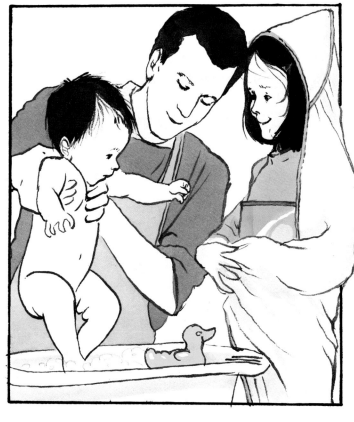

33 and dodge the splashes

34 dry him

35 dress him

36 brush his hair

37 kiss him better

38 whisper a secret

39 tickle his tummy

40 and give him some toys

watch out for . . .

41 hair pulling

42 nose grabbing

43 dribbling

44 and drooling

45 watch out for shoe sucking

46 letter eating

47 ankle biting

48 head banging

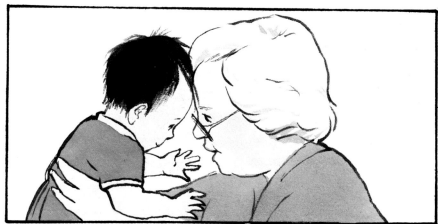

49 and watch out for Granny's glasses

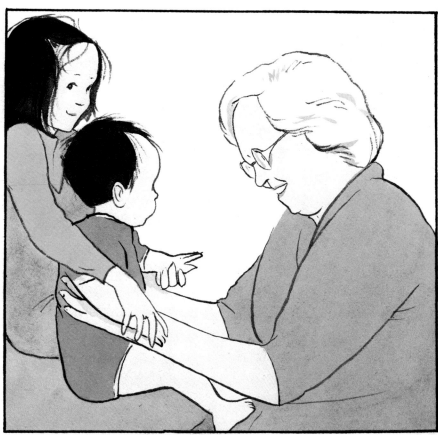

50 hang out the washing

51 rock baby to sleep

52 shoo away the cat

53 make a daisy chain

54 and look out for rain

55 bring the washing in again

56 hide

57 play peepo

58 say boo

59 try on Mother's hat

60 or Father's shoes

61 put him in his cot for a quiet time

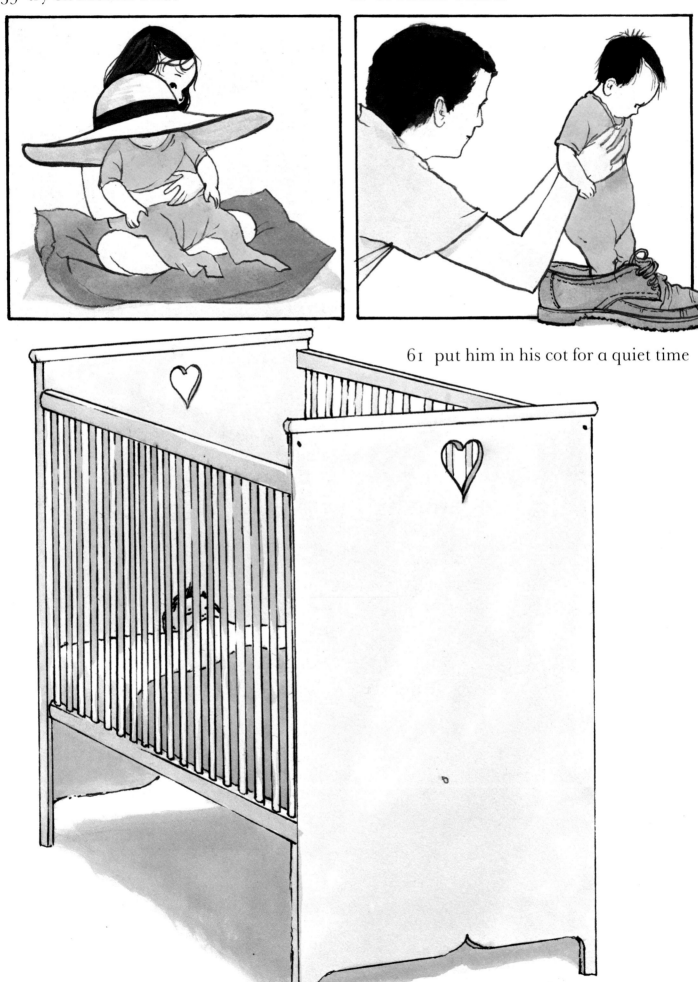

62 dress up in his wrap

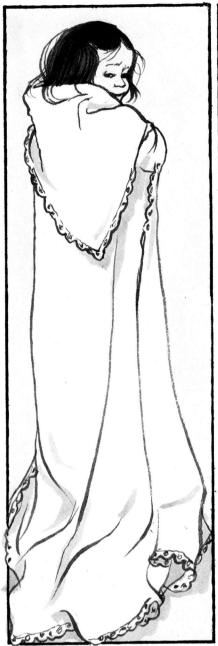

63 play with his teddy

64 build with his blocks

65 or borrow his basket

until he wakes up again

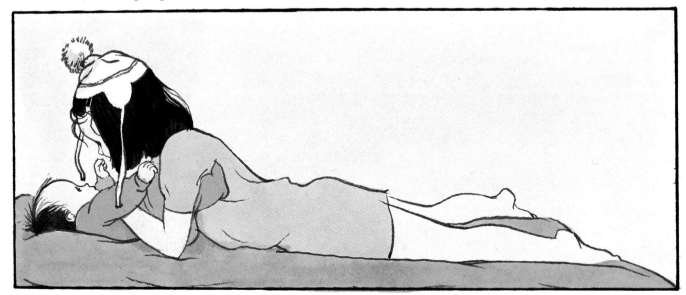

66 touch his nose

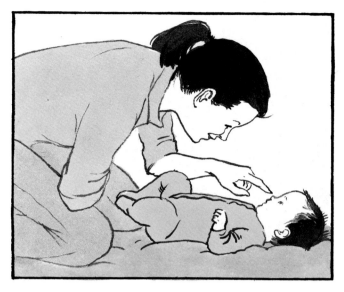

67 walk up from his toes

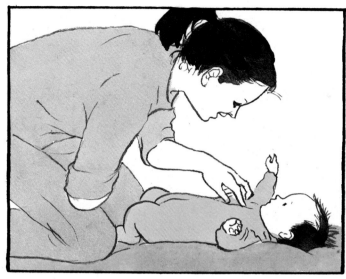

68 kiss his ear or

69 blow on his tummy

70 take him for a slow stroll

71 or a fast roll

72 take him in the car

73 or take him on a picnic

74 carry him on your knee   75 or like this   76 like this

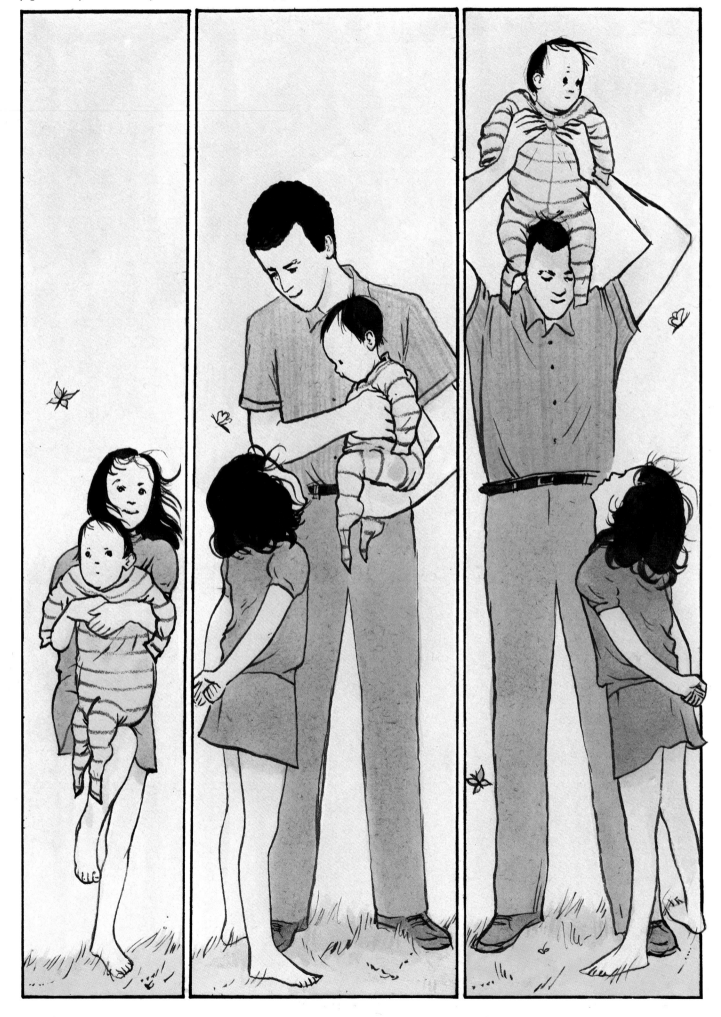

80 collect rocks

81 leaves

82 bugs

83 and flowers for him

but not to eat

84 let him meet big dogs

85 babies

86 snails

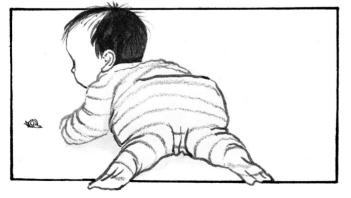

87 and fish

88 roll him up in a rug

 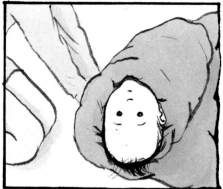 

89 make him a baby box

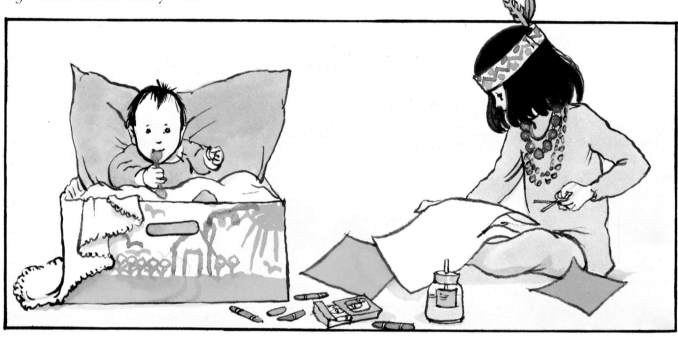

90 take him into your tent with you

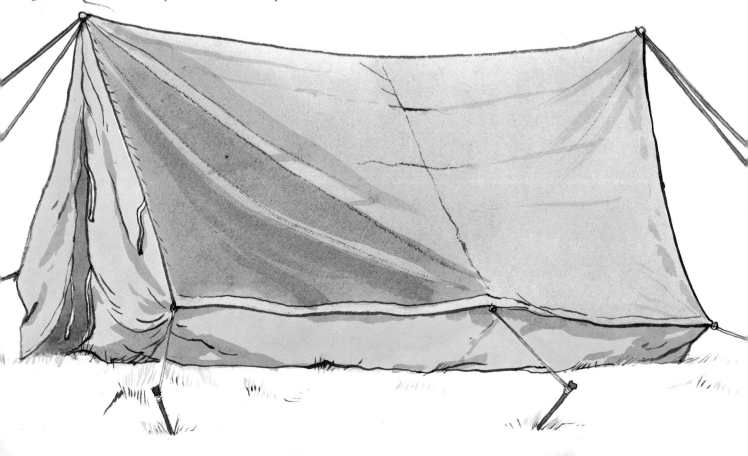

91 try him in his bouncing chair

92 try him with a book

93 try him with some rattling toys

94 or let him sit with you

95 watch television together

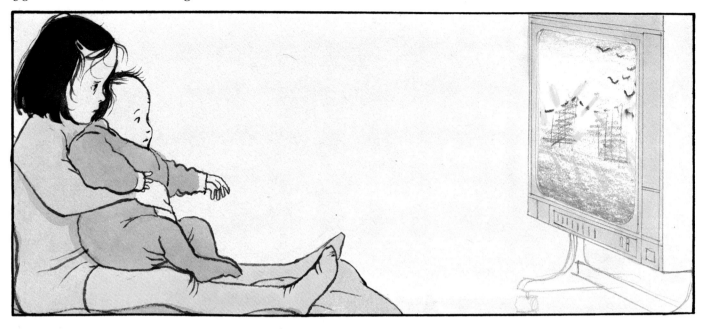

until he's bored

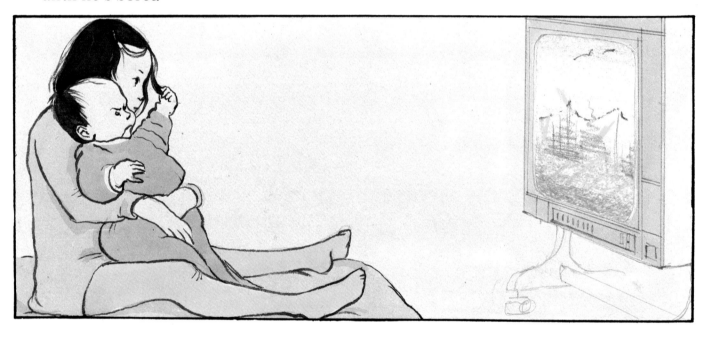

96 give him a book to read

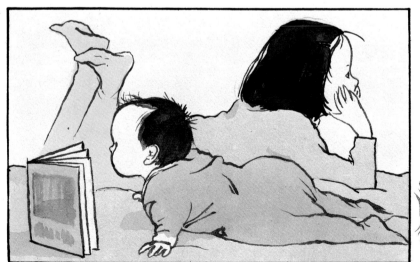

97 but not to chew or tear

98 shout at him

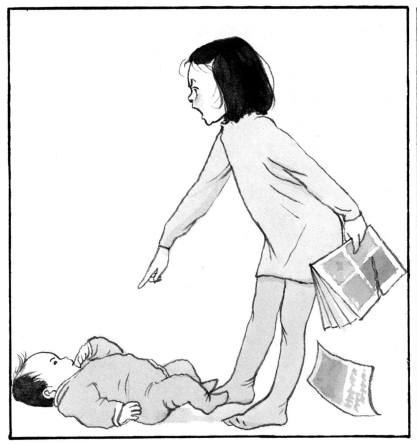

99 and make him cry

100 give him a cuddle

101 and a kiss good night

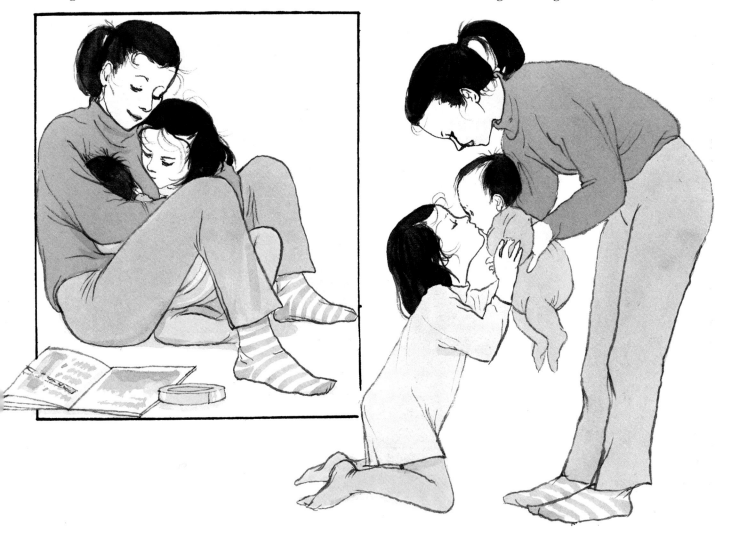

EDUCATION

Pre Sch - Gr 3
babies
new baby
jealousy

1984